CANADA

Minnesota

Wisconsin

Michigan

Iowa

Illinois

Indiana

Ohio

Missouri

Kansas

Kentucky

West Virginia

Virginia

Oklahoma

Arkansas

Tennessee

North Carolina

Mississippi

Alabama

Georgia

South Carolina

Louisiana

Texas

Florida

New Hampshire

Vermont

Maine

New York

Pennsylvania

Massachusetts

Rhode Island

Connecticut

New Jersey

Delaware

Maryland

Washington, D.C.

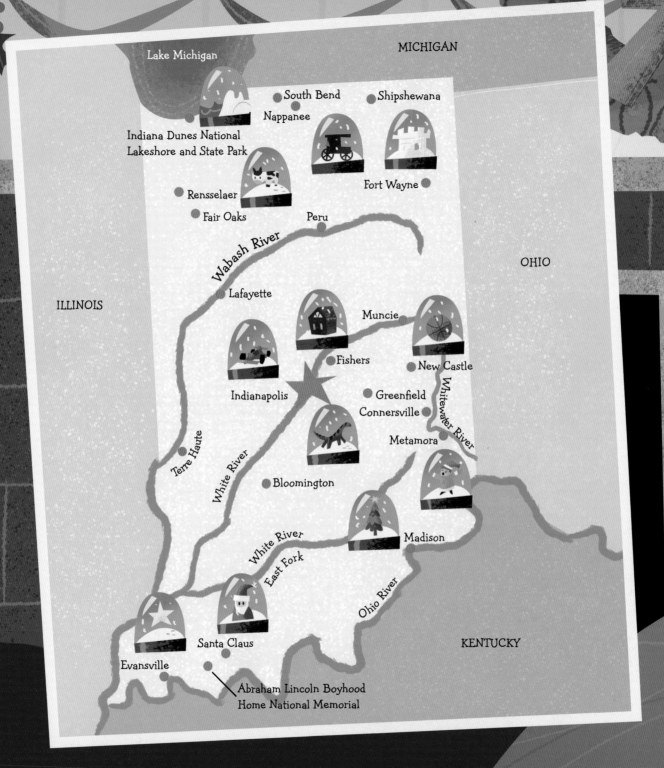

MICHIGAN

Lake Michigan

South Bend

Shipshewana

Nappanee

Indiana Dunes National
Lakeshore and State Park

Fort Wayne

Rensselaer

Fair Oaks

Peru

Wabash River

OHIO

ILLINOIS

Lafayette

Muncie

Fishers

New Castle

Whitewater River

Indianapolis

Greenfield

Connersville

Terre Haute

White River

Metamora

Bloomington

White River

East Fork

Madison

Ohio River

Santa Claus

KENTUCKY

Evansville

Abraham Lincoln Boyhood
Home National Memorial

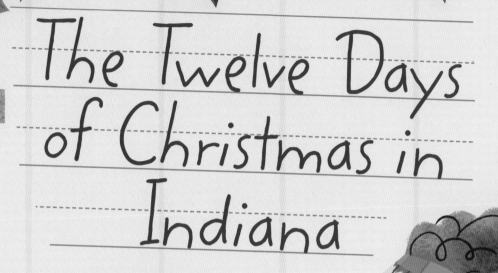

The Twelve Days of Christmas in Indiana

written by
Donna Griffin

illustrated by
Troy Cummings

STERLING CHILDREN'S BOOKS
New York

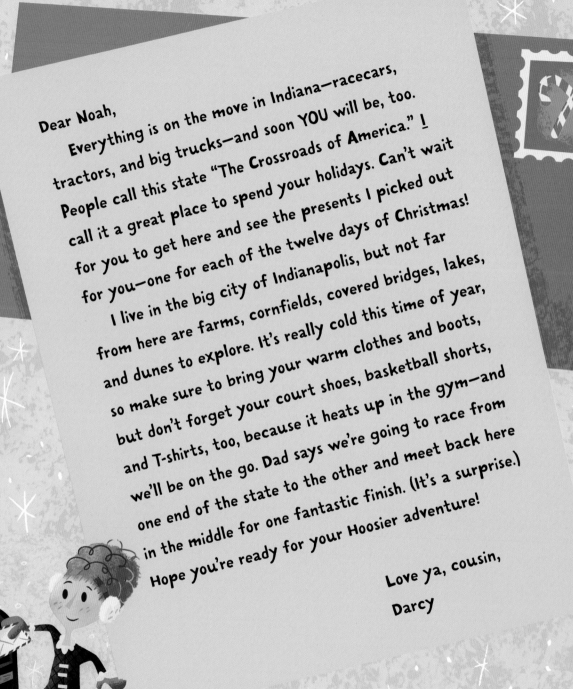

Dear Noah,

Everything is on the move in Indiana—racecars, tractors, and big trucks—and soon YOU will be, too. People call this state "The Crossroads of America." I call it a great place to spend your holidays. Can't wait for you to get here and see the presents I picked out for you—one for each of the twelve days of Christmas!

I live in the big city of Indianapolis, but not far from here are farms, cornfields, covered bridges, lakes, and dunes to explore. It's really cold this time of year, so make sure to bring your warm clothes and boots, but don't forget your court shoes, basketball shorts, and T-shirts, too, because it heats up in the gym—and we'll be on the go. Dad says we're going to race from one end of the state to the other and meet back here in the middle for one fantastic finish. (It's a surprise.)

Hope you're ready for your Hoosier adventure!

Love ya, cousin,
Darcy

Dear Mom and Dad,

I'm still catching my breath from my first day in Indiana. Aunt Lynn, Uncle Dave, Darcy, and I drove straight from the Indianapolis airport to Madison, a small town on the Ohio River where Uncle Dave grew up.

It was major Christmas overload as we walked through the Festival of Trees. There were more than a HUNDRED trees—each with different decorations. Imagine all the room for presents! My favorite was the tulip tree—Indiana's state tree. One of the ornaments hanging from its branches was a bright red bird. Just as I was turning to look at the next tree, the ornament flapped its wings! It was a real bird!

Darcy didn't seem surprised—she explained that it was a cardinal, Indiana's state bird. I know it sounds crazy, but he was wearing a coach's cap and a tiny whistle around his neck . . . so I named him Coach. As we walked along the riverfront, Coach followed us, fluttering from tree to tree.

Aunt Lynn says there's a lot of history in Madison's riverfront, where old steamboats still travel up and down the Ohio River. But the boats everyone comes to watch now are a lot faster. Madison's biggest festival is the annual Madison Regatta in July with hydroplane boat races, air shows, and even fireworks. I'm definitely on board for a return trip this summer!

Love,
Noah

On the first day of Christmas,
my cousin gave to me . . .

a cardinal in a
tulip tree.

Dear Mom and Dad,

Today I found out what "Hoosier Hysteria" is all about and no, it's not about crazy people—although basketball fans in Indiana are pretty loud and proud of their teams. At the Indiana Basketball Hall of Fame in New Castle, we checked out jerseys and trophies and learned a ton about some of the great Indiana basketball players—Larry Bird, Oscar Robertson, and John Wooden. Even better, Darcy and I found a spot where we could take the game-winning shot and call plays just like real sportscasters!

Coach is one bossy bird. He kept chirping and pecking on my head until I followed him into New Castle High School's gym next door. It's the world's largest high school basketball gym—absolutely HUGE!

"Run the picket fence, Bobby, and don't get caught watching the paint dry!" Darcy yelled. She loves to quote from the movie <u>Hoosiers,</u> which is based on the true story of tiny Milan High School that won the State Basketball Championship in 1954. Indiana basketball is full of legends that prove miracles happen.

Darcy and I took home our own basketballs so we can keep practicing our moves.

As the coach said in <u>Hoosiers</u> . . .
"I love you guys,"
Noah

On the second day of Christmas,
my cousin gave to me . . .

2 bouncing balls

and a cardinal in a tulip tree.

Dear Mom and Dad,

What's up, you ask? Well, thanks to today's adventures at the Koch Planetarium, I know a lot more about what's up . . . in the winter night sky that is!

The planetarium, which is inside the Evansville Museum of Arts, History and Science, is the oldest one in the state—visitors here have been gazing at the stars and planets for 60 years. Now there is a brand-new full dome for a 360-degree view of the whole sky.

Did you know one of the biggest constellations you can see during the winter months is Orion the Hunter? During a planetarium show, we learned about the bright collection of stars that appears in the eastern sky just after the sun goes down. Here's how we found it: Look for three bright stars in a row—that's Orion's belt. Around the belt is a rectangle made of four stars. Betelgeuse and Rigel in the opposite corners of the rectangle are two of the brightest stars in the sky—perfect for a special Christmas wish.

Even though I may not be able to see you right now, Mom and Dad, we are under the same sky. Look up and see our three bright stars tonight. I will, too!

Love,
Noah

ORION!

On the third day of Christmas, my cousin gave to me . . .

3 bright stars

2 bouncing balls,
and a cardinal in a tulip tree.

Dear Mom and Dad,

You can call me Farmer Noah now. I've seen big barns, silos, tractors, horses, and cows everywhere we've traveled. Farms are an important part of Indiana life—corn and soybeans are the two main crops in the state. Since it's winter and there are no crops growing, we drove to Fair Oaks Farms to see dairy cows. (Aunt Lynn grew up on a farm and she wanted us to see one in action.)

We rode to the milking parlor in a big bus painted to look like a cow. But what we saw next was even weirder than the bus: 72 cows riding a wacky merry-go-round that's really a machine that milks them three times a day. We practiced hooking up a cow statue to a milking machine while Coach kept track of our times. Neither one of us could beat the time it takes the staff at Fair Oaks to hook up a real cow (only 19 seconds!), but Darcy was a little faster than me. Don't worry, I'll beat her next time.

The best part of the trip was celebrating the birthday of Christy the calf. Every day, 80 to 100 calves are born at Fair Oaks, but Christy was the most special of them all to us because we got to see her being born. It was amazing (and, yeah, a little gross).

Now I really feel like a COW-boy!

Love,
Noah

On the fourth day of Christmas,
my cousin gave to me . . .

A mooing cows

3 bright stars, 2 bouncing balls,
and a cardinal in a tulip tree.

Dear Mom and Dad,

Today we kept driving north till we came to the northern edge of Indiana and got stopped by Lake Michigan. Indiana may not have mountains or an ocean, but this Great Lake and the nearby dunes are fantastic!

Uncle Dave had a special treat in store for us—an airplane tour of the dunes. In just an hour, we flew over open beaches and 200-foot dunes sprinkled with the shrubs, trees, and prairies that make up Indiana Dunes State Park. At one point on our bird's-eye ride over the dunes, we met some of Coach's friends: five American goldfinches who performed a perfect flying V next to our plane!

The American goldfinch is one of the 352 types of birds that live in the Dunes. There are 46 species of mammals, 18 species of amphibians, 23 species of reptiles, 71 species of fish, 60 species of butterflies, and 60 species of dragonflies and damselflies found here. You can see them by hiking and bird-watching all year round, and in the winter you can explore on snowshoes or skis—Darcy says the dunes are great for swooshing and zooming!

Your high-flying son,
Noah

Dear Mom and Dad,

We're still on the move—just a little slower now. This morning we stopped at Nappanee, a tiny Amish town in the northwest part of the state. <u>Clip-clop, clip-clop</u>—we followed the sound to a horse-drawn buggy pulling into the McDonald's drive-thru! Downtown Nappanee has hitching racks and buggy sheds alongside parking lots and car garages. The Amish community believes in a simple life, where traditions are preserved through hard work and without modern technology. We visited one of the oldest Amish farms in Indiana called Amish Acres, complete with barnyard hens, livestock, gardens, and an apple orchard. We sampled some of the homemade pies and cakes, and Aunt Lynn stocked up on noodles, raisin bread, and shoofly pie (don't worry—it's made with molasses, not flies). She also bought a log cabin quilt to keep us warm on the drive home.

At the Wagon Shed, Darcy bought a bonnet and I bought some cool britches and a hat before we took our own Amish buggy ride, bouncing down the gravel lane around the farm pond and through the woods. The buggy stopped at a one-room schoolhouse built in the 1870s. There was even a horse-drawn school bus waiting outside! Inside the school, we checked out the wood stove, cloakrooms, lunch buckets, and desks. The school marm gave us each a tablet to sign before we left—at least she didn't give us homework.

You bet your britches—I had lots of fun!

Love,
Noah

On the sixth day of Christmas,
my cousin gave to me . . .

6 Amish buggies

5 golden birds, 4 mooing cows, 3 bright stars, 2 bouncing balls,
and a cardinal in a tulip tree.

Dear Mom and Dad,

Today we headed south and east to Connersville for a special train ride and guess what? I got to wear my pajamas for the whole day! All the kids were in pj's to ride the Polar Express train that took us through the countryside for a holiday trip and a visit to St. Nick. Then we took another train to Metamora, a town famous for its annual Christmas Walk.

Metamora is the only working canal town in Indiana, with a big grist mill that grinds cornmeal and flour. Aunt Lynn called the town a "Christmas wonderland"— and she was right! There were lanterns shining on the Whitewater Canal, twinkling lights in all the shop windows, and Christmas carolers singing "Jingle Bells."

The carolers waved to us, and Coach started chirping like crazy. I'm pretty sure he was saying, "It's no fun to just listen; let's join them." Darcy was shy but I gave her a little cousinly push and told her I'd be right behind her. We caught up with the group just in time for my favorite song, "We Wish You a Merry Christmas." When we rode the train back to Connersville, I was a little hoarse but a definite believer in the spirit of Christmas.

Jingling all the way,
Noah

P.S. In Metamora, from May to October, you can ride the Ben Franklin III, a boat pulled by horses down the Whitewater Canal and across the only wood aqueduct in the country. Darcy says we have to come back in October for the Canal Days Festival. Mark your calendar!

Dear Mom and Dad,

What weighs 15 tons but could disappear in a day? Answer: ice sculptures! Luckily it's cold enough outside here in Indiana that the sculptures at the Shipshewana Ice Festival will stick around longer than that.

When we arrived in Shipshewana, we saw that artists had already created ice wreaths, animals, toys, and a nativity scene to decorate businesses all over town. While we waited for the main ice sculpting competition to begin, Aunt Lynn bought us snowman pins as entry tickets so we could try the samples at the Chili Cook-Off. I'm pretty sure the hot spices burned off all of my taste buds!

Finally, it was time . . . all the ice sculptors took their marks in front of more than 30,000 pounds of ice blocks to shape their creations. We watched them shave, saw, and drill for hours—it was pretty slow work. But then, just like magic, the plain old ice blocks were transformed into a reindeer, an angel, a giraffe, a castle, and even a bird that Coach was sure looked just like him. Darcy and I found a small leftover ice block, so we tried making our own ice sculpture. We chipped out a circle shape to make a wreath, and Coach volunteered to be our decoration.

We didn't win an award, but Uncle Dave said our creation would make a great hood ornament.

Love,
Noah

On the eighth day of Christmas,
my cousin gave to me . . .

8 sculptures
sparkling

7 singers strolling, 6 Amish buggies, 5 golden birds,
4 mooing cows, 3 bright stars, 2 bouncing balls,
and a cardinal in a tulip tree.

Dear Mom and Dad,

Darcy's state may be almost 3,500 miles from the North Pole, but you can find Christmas every day in Santa Claus, Indiana. Darcy and I counted the Christmas lights as we drove through town, and Aunt Lynn took a photo of us next to the giant Santa statue.

At Santa's Candy Castle, machines clinked and whirred as they popped out candy of all colors and kinds. We chatted online with elves on computers connected to the North Pole. Both Darcy and I got certificates showing we are on Santa's Good List. (Told you so.)

All this activity made us hungry, and we followed the smell to the chestnuts roasting on an open fire . . . just like in the song! I actually tried one. It was sweet and tasted kind of like butter.

As we left the town of Santa Claus, we drove by a log cabin exactly like the one Abraham Lincoln lived in when he was a boy. Just think—he was about <u>my</u> age when he lived in Indiana. Hard to imagine President Lincoln as a kid. Do you think he was on Santa's Good List back then?

Love,
Noah

On the ninth day of Christmas,
my cousin gave to me . . .

9 chestnuts roasting

8 sculptures sparkling, 7 singers strolling, 6 Amish buggies,
5 golden birds, 4 mooing cows, 3 bright stars, 2 bouncing balls,
and a cardinal in a tulip tree.

Dear Mom and Dad,

Today we found out what being a pioneer was really like when we traveled back in time at Conner Prairie Interactive History Park in Fishers. Darcy and I took a wagon ride to the animal barn to find out how the cows, sheep, and chickens stay warm in the winter. Residents of Prairietown shared their holiday traditions and invited us to make a gingerbread house for the Gingerbread Village. Ours looked a lot like Lucas Oil Stadium where the Indianapolis Colts play. Everyone got to vote for the best gingerbread creation, and I think we scored a touchdown!

Tonight we had a special dinner at Conner Prairie—a hearthside supper. We helped cook our own food in the fireplace: I rolled the fried potato balls, and Darcy baked a squash pie. Then we sat down to a candlelight feast—just like in 1836. Boy, I'm stuffed.

Love,
Noah

P.S. There's even more to explore at Conner Prairie in warmer weather—we can fly up, up, and away in a balloon ride just like the one that first took place in 1859. The history park is also going to have rocket launches, camps, and SpaceLabs at the new Spaceport center.

On the tenth day of Christmas, my cousin gave to me . . .

10 tasty houses

9 chestnuts roasting, 8 sculptures sparkling,
7 singers strolling, 6 Amish buggies, 5 golden birds, 4 mooing cows,
3 bright stars, 2 bouncing balls, and a cardinal in a tulip tree.

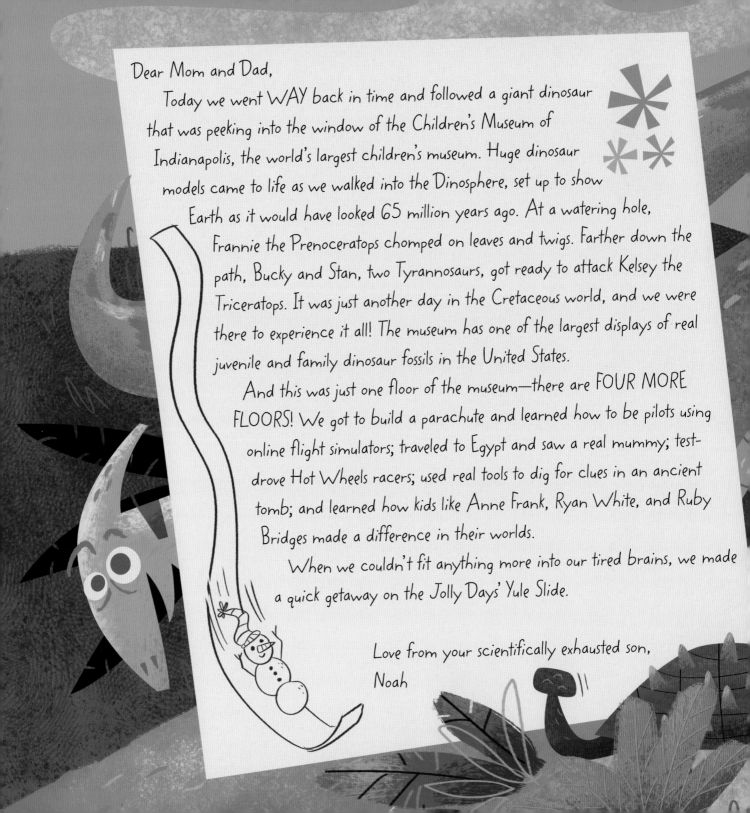

Dear Mom and Dad,

Today we went WAY back in time and followed a giant dinosaur that was peeking into the window of the Children's Museum of Indianapolis, the world's largest children's museum. Huge dinosaur models came to life as we walked into the Dinosphere, set up to show Earth as it would have looked 65 million years ago. At a watering hole, Frannie the Prenoceratops chomped on leaves and twigs. Farther down the path, Bucky and Stan, two Tyrannosaurs, got ready to attack Kelsey the Triceratops. It was just another day in the Cretaceous world, and we were there to experience it all! The museum has one of the largest displays of real juvenile and family dinosaur fossils in the United States.

And this was just one floor of the museum—there are FOUR MORE FLOORS! We got to build a parachute and learned how to be pilots using online flight simulators; traveled to Egypt and saw a real mummy; test-drove Hot Wheels racers; used real tools to dig for clues in an ancient tomb; and learned how kids like Anne Frank, Ryan White, and Ruby Bridges made a difference in their worlds.

When we couldn't fit anything more into our tired brains, we made a quick getaway on the Jolly Days' Yule Slide.

Love from your scientifically exhausted son,
Noah

Dear Mom and Dad,

Holidays in Indianapolis center around Monument Circle, which gets turned into the world's largest Christmas tree every year. It's not a <u>real</u> tree at all, but strings of lights that stretch from the ground to the top of the monument, which is almost 300 feet tall. There's nothing like climbing the stairs of the monument, looking up from underneath at the Christmas lights, and twirling around like Darcy and I did. (Yes, I got a little dizzy.)

Next we drove a few miles to the west side of the city. I wasn't sure what Uncle Dave meant when he said we would see where the greatest spectacle in racing was held, but now I know. Every May, the Indy 500 packs more than 250,000 people into the stands!

Normally, you can tour the speedway track in a bus that goes a lot slower than the 220 miles per hour that Indy cars travel. But today was a special day. We followed Coach to the pits where the race cars were revving up for four turns around the two-and-a-half mile oval.

Guess what? Darcy and I got to wave the checkered flags to get the race started—best surprise ever!

We couldn't tell who had won the race, but no one cared. We all lined up to kiss the bricks at the end, just like the drivers and their crews do after they win.

Now I'm heading down the home straightaway. Do you think you could rent a truck at the airport when you pick me up tomorrow? Darcy gave me some pretty amazing presents.

Love,
Noah

On the twelfth day of Christmas,
my cousin gave to me . . .

12 cars a-racing

11 dinos roaming, 10 tasty houses, 9 chestnuts roasting,
8 sculptures sparkling, 7 singers strolling, 6 Amish buggies,
5 golden birds, 4 mooing cows, 3 bright stars, 2 bouncing balls,
and a cardinal in a tulip tree.

INDIANA: RACING CAPITAL OF THE WORLD!

Indiana: The Hoosier State

State Capital: Indianapolis • **State Abbreviation:** IN • **State Bird:** the northern cardinal • **State Tree:** the tulip poplar • **State Flower:** the peony • **State Stone:** Salem limestone • **State Motto:** "The Crossroads of America" • **State Poem:** "Indiana," by Arthur Franklin Mapes • **State Song:** "On the Banks of the Wabash, Far Away," by Paul Dresser

Some Famous Hoosiers:

Larry Bird (1956–), born in West Baden Springs, took his Indiana State University team to the NCAA Finals in 1979. His rivalry with Magic Johnson made the championship game the most-watched college game in the history of televised basketball. Bird played 13 seasons with the Boston Celtics, leading his team to three NBA championships. He became the head coach for the Indiana Pacers, then team president. He is the only person to be named the NBA's MVP, Coach of the Year, and Executive of the Year.

Meg Cabot (1967–), born in Bloomington, is the award-winning author of more than fifty books. She is best known for *The Princess Diaries* series, which chronicles the escapades of Mia, the Princess of Genovia. Two feature-length movies have been adapted from the books.

Michael Jackson (1958–2009) was born in Gary and, as a child, was the lead singer in The Jackson Five, a band he formed with his older brothers. Later, as a solo artist, he recorded many hits, including "Thriller," "Billie Jean," and "Rock With You." He broke attendance and sales records and rose to be the King of Pop, an international icon, changing music and influencing generations of artists to come.

David Letterman (1947–), born in Indianapolis, took his quirky Hoosier humor to New York, with his *Late Night with David Letterman* show in 1982 and then his *Late Show with David Letterman*. He has donated millions of dollars to Indianapolis-based organizations as well as to his alma mater, Ball State University, in Muncie. A building on campus is named after him: the David Letterman Communication and Media Building.

Jane Pauley (1950–), born in Indianapolis, became a leading broadcast journalist. She was co-host of the *Today* show at twenty-five, helped launch *Dateline NBC*, and hosted *The Jane Pauley Show*. She currently works to promote mental health, children's health, and education.

Oscar Robertson (1938–) grew up in Indianapolis. While attending Crispus Attucks High School he attracted national attention by leading the Tigers to a 45-game winning streak—they were the first African American team to win two consecutive Indiana state basketball titles. For his achievements in college and professional basketball, Robertson was named "Player of the Century" by the National Association of Basketball Coaches in 2000.

To my children, Dani, Darcy, and David, who make all my days special with their love, intelligence, compassion, and humor; to Noah and Portia Danielle, the true gifts and inspirations of my life; and to my husband, Dave, for always seeing me as your high school sweetheart. To Mom and Dad, thanks for instilling in me stubborn Hoosier pride, common sense, and the belief I can achieve my dreams.
—D.G.

To Hardrock, Coco, and Joe.
—T.C.

STERLING CHILDREN'S BOOKS
New York

An Imprint of Sterling Publishing
387 Park Avenue South
New York, NY 10016

Text © 2014 by Donna Griffin
Illustrations © 2014 by Troy Cummings

The original illustrations for this book were created in pencil, and then painted digitally.
Designed by Ellen Duda

ISBN 978-1-4549-0888-3

Library of Congress Cataloging-in-Publication Data

Griffin, Donna.
  The twelve days of Christmas in Indiana / by Donna Griffin ; illustrated by Troy Cummings.
    pages cm
  Summary: Noah writes a letter home each of the twelve days he spends exploring the state of Indiana at Christmastime, as his cousin Darcy shows him everything from the world's largest Christmas tree to the Indianapolis Motor Speedway. Includes facts about Indiana.
  ISBN 978-1-4549-0888-3
  [1. Indiana--Fiction. 2. Christmas--Fiction. 3. Cousins--Fiction. 4. Letters--Fiction.] I. Cummings, Troy, illustrator. II. Title.
  PZ7.G881328Twe 2014
  [Fic]--dc23
                                                                                        2013040036

Distributed in Canada by Sterling Publishing
c/o Canadian Manda Group, 165 Dufferin Street
Toronto, Ontario, Canada M6K 3H6
Distributed in the United Kingdom by GMC Distribution Services
Castle Place, 166 High Street, Lewes, East Sussex, England BN7 1XU
Distributed in Australia by Capricorn Link (Australia) Pty. Ltd.
P.O. Box 704, Windsor, NSW 2756, Australia

For information about custom editions, special sales, and premium and corporate purchases, please contact
Sterling Special Sales at 800-805-5489 or specialsales@sterlingpublishing.com.

Manufactured in China
Lot #:
2 4 6 8 10 9 7 5 3 1
07/14

www.sterlingpublishing.com/kids

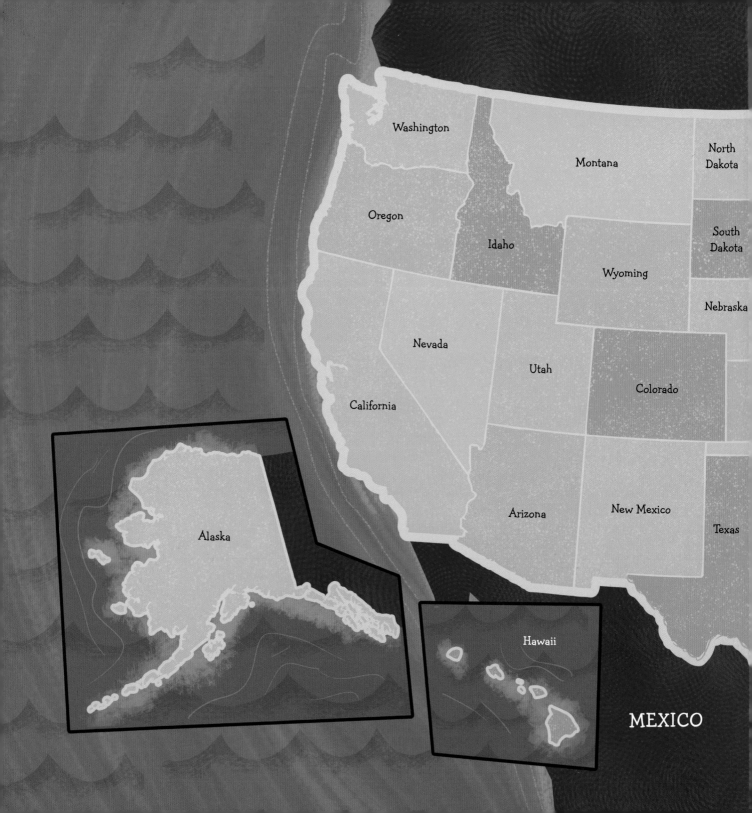